Dream Grabber

Written by John R. Green

Illustrated by Susan Shorter

Archway Publishing books may be ordered through booksellers or by contacting:

Archway Publishing
1663 Liberty Drive
Bloomington, IN 47403
www.archwaypublishing.com
1 (888) 242-5904

Illustrations by Susan Shorter.

ISBN: 978-1-4808-9477-8 (sc)
ISBN: 978-1-4808-9475-4 (hc)
ISBN: 978-1-4808-9476-1 (e)

Printed in the United States of America.

Archway Publishing rev. date: 10/6/2020

To
Anthony,
Francesca,
and
A.J.,
who fill my heart
with love

W

hen it's time for A.J.
to go to bed,
He'd rather do anything
else instead,

Like ride a bike or watch TV.
He'd even rather climb a tree.

You see, A.J. doesn't like to sleep. In fact, bedtime often makes him weep.

Even when Grandma
reads him a book,
He lies there with this
terrible look,

Worried about dreams that could scare him at night. Dreams may not all be bad, but some might.

Dada tells A.J. there's
no reason to fear
"Because I have a secret
that I have held dear.

Dada has the power to
see here in bed
The dreams already hiding
inside your head."

"But with a rub of my hands
and your eyes shut tight,
I can grab those bad dreams
that would give you a fright."

"I see one on top, and
another right here.
There's even a third
hiding inside your ear."

"I crush them really hard
inside my fist,
Then throw them toward space
where they won't be missed."

A.J. asks, "But what
will I dream now if
I go to sleep?
Are there good dreams
inside I still get to keep?"

"There are," Dada says.
"I see them quite clearly.
But that's not all I see,
dear A.J.—not nearly."

"Dada can also see good
dreams floating in air
And grab them with the same
hands that got rid of the scare."

"These good dreams I see I
will hold very lightly
And give them to you if you
close your eyes tightly.
In they go now in your
head where they'll stay,
Filling your sleep in the
most beautiful way."

"With stories of fun and happy times only, Now when you dream you'll never be lonely Because Dada put those dreams in your head To help you feel good about going to bed."

"With love and a kiss that
you get to keep
And a smile on your
face as you fall asleep."

Acknowledgments

Many thanks to Lori Greiner for your friendship, and for encouraging me to write this book.

To Robin Roberts, Samantha Chapman and Gabriel Kerr for your incredible support and enthusiasm.

To my 1st grade teacher Christine Williams, who nurtured my passion for reading and writing at Old Bonhomme Elementary School in St. Louis.

To Anthony La Bate for your patience and creativity.

And to Francesca and A.J. for inspiring me to DREAM big.

About the Author

John R. Green is a multiple Emmy and Peabody Award winning television news and documentary writer and producer. He is a 25 year veteran of ABC News and currently serves as Executive Producer of Special Programming there, as well as Executive Vice President of Rock'n Robin Productions, a full service production company based in New York City. In addition to writing his first kids' book *Dream Grabber* based on real bed time rituals he created to help his own young children face their bedtime fears, Green authored *Dream Jumper*, a companion book for parents and children. Green and his husband Anthony live in suburban New Jersey with their twins Francesca and A.J.

Learn more at TimeToDreamBooks.com

Draw Your Dreams

Draw Your Dreams

Draw Your Dreams